NO PRISONERS TAKEN

William Agunwa

Polyverse Publications
Carpinteria, CA United States

By the same author:

A Shadowed Dawn
Jobs for the Boys
Love's Mirror: A Tragic Romance

To Gudrun, Nicky, and Johnny

NO PRISONERS TAKEN

1

'Sani Abacha dead! And no shots fired in anger. Sex-pistolled! The Viagra swinger flat out for good in his Abuja Aso Rock bunker – he did not have the stamina to last the course with those feisty call-girls *a trois*!'

Peter Ofondu reasoned that he couldn't have come back to Nigeria at a better time. His attempt to take his life after the Biafran war by shooting himself in the right temple with his Biafran-made pistol in Gonzo had resulted in severe splitting headaches. The delirium he had suffered earlier during the *felenza* – influenza – crisis had affected his trigger finger. He had in fact only grazed his right temple with the bullet and lost consciousness briefly.

From Gonzo Peter Ofondu eventually found his way to Douala in the Cameroons, where he caught a flight to Abidjan in the Ivory Coast and thence to London. It was now August 1998, and he had returned to Nigeria via Lagos. He had been advised by friends not to travel to Nigeria; the military might still be interested in him because of his prominent part in the Biafran war and his subsequent escape to Gonzo. But he felt compelled to see his father, troubled by the reported 'accident' that had befallen him.

Nigeria had been in turmoil following the 12th June 1993 Presidential election, which Chief Moshood Abiola was supposed to have won. But the military under General Babangida

overruled the result and Abiola was
subsequently imprisoned by General Abacha
(The Butcher), only to die in custody in July
1998, just before General Abacha's own curious
death.

Peter soon realized that he was in fact
there for the burial ceremonies of his father, a
titled Chief in his eighties. His car had
accidentally been caught in the crossfire of a
brutal gangland feud involving a mafia type
syndicate, called the 4-1-9 after the Nigerian
Advanced Free Fraud Criminal Code Section
419.

These extortionist and murderous gangs
and organized syndicates were rampant and
were a law unto themselves under the anarchic
regime of General Sani Abacha, who was

believed to have stolen some $4 billion, as much

of it directly from the Central Bank, as well as

bribes from foreign contractors. The Swiss

Federal Banking Commission later froze $600

million in deposits and repatriated some of these

funds to Nigeria. The Financial Services

Authority (FSA) in the UK revealed that 23

banks in the UK had handled $1.3 billion of

Abacha hot money in the Nigerian pillage. The

Jersey Financial Services Commission also

found bank accounts used by associates of

General Abacha at five of Jersey's 600-plus

financial institutions.

As soon as Peter Ofondu arrived at

Lagos airport in August 1998 via Paris (direct

London to Nigeria flights then were rare,

following the international isolation of the brutal

military dictatorship of General Sani Abacha that had cold-bloodedly executed, among others, the Ogoni-land activist, Ken Saro-Wiwa), he began to analyze and absorb the social and economic situation as best he could.

For a change, Lagos Murtala Muhammed International Airport seemed like a normal airport with orderly queues, no threatening harassment from touts, and the baggage carousels were functioning! There was a semblance of discipline, and less edginess about the behavior of airport official or the dreaded state security service (SSS). This was in marked contrast to what had seen when he arrived at dilapidate Kano International Airport in 1993 before flying to Lagos to catch a connecting internal flight to Enugu. The military presence seemed far less oppressive under the

new military leader, General Abdulsalam

Abubakar, who kept his promise and handed

over the reins of power peacefully to the

democratically elected civilian administration of

ex-General Obasanjo.

2

On Monday the 20th of July 1998, the new

military head of State, General Abubakar, in a

national broadcast, signaled a change of mood

and attitude of the military:

'It is quite clear from the efforts we have

made to reach out to the people that

Nigerians want nothing less than true

democracy in a united and peaceful

country. It is clear that Nigerians want a

country where fairness, justice and equity

are not mere slogans, but principles put

into timely and indiscriminate practice.

Nigerians want true democracy which

must be based on a sound democratic foundation to ensure fulfillment and sustenance… The administration is concerned about the level of corruption in our national life. Such concern emanates from lapses in the management of public funds … Drugs and advance fee fraud, among other syndicate crimes remain an embarrassment to the nation. We therefore commit ourselves to enter into necessary co-operation with all nations to fight these for our mutual benefit…

After all necessary consultation, government has decided that the election of a civilian president will be held in the first quarter of 1999. The newly elected President will be sworn into office on the

29th of May 1999. We trust that we shall

all work towards building bridges of

understanding and respect for one

another.'

He had also announced that the Provisional

Ruling Council had granted pardon to General

Olusegun Obasanjo and posthumously to late

Major-General Shehu Musa Yar'Adua (he died

in prison), who were convicted of an alleged

coup plot in 1995.

'Yes,' Peter mused. 'I'll put my money

on General Obasanjo being the next President: a

good bridge between the old military and the

new civilian regime. He was after all the only

military ruler to hand over power voluntarily to

a civilian government. But again you can never

be too sure about even ex-Generals when they

taste absolute power. Old habits die hard. In

these tricky circumstances one would just have

to wait and see.'

When General Murtala Ramat

Muhammed was assassinated in Lagos in a state

car on the 13th of February 1976, his right-hand

man then was the Chief of Staff, Supreme

Headquarters. Lieutenant-General Olusegun

Obasanjo. He became the next Head of State

and Commander-in-Chief of the Armed Forces.

He set out to pursue the policies that he and his

predecessor had laid down, namely to clean

society, to restore its dignity, to arrest the

deteriorating state of the economy brought

about, among other things, by a slump in the oil

market and to return the country to civilian rule in 1979.

The highlights of this regime included the launching of Operation Feed the Nation in 1976, a bold attempt to boost agriculture and self-sufficiency; the launching of the Universal Primary Education Scheme (UPE) to make a primary education free and universal in September 1976; and the introduction of a National Pledge of Loyalty to be recited by pupils at the beginning and end of every school day, and at every major assembly. The Pledge of September 1976 read:

I pledge to Nigeria my country
To be faithful, loyal, and honest,
To serve Nigeria with all my
strength,
To defend her unity and uphold
her honour and glory,
So help me God.

He also introduced the National Honours Award

for deserving persons in recognition of their

service to the nation in March 1977; and the

adoption of a new National Anthem in 1978:

Arise, O compatriots, Nigeria call obey

To serve our Fatherland

With love and strength and faith

The labour of our heroes past,

Shall never be in vain:

To serve with heart and might

One nation bound in freedom, peace

and unity

Oh God of Creation, direct our noble

cause,

Guide our Leaders right,

Help our Youth the truth to know.

In love and honesty to grow,

And living just and true

Great lofty heights attain,

To build a nation where peace and

justice shall reign.

The major achievement of General Obasanjo's regime was the transition to civilian rule, with elections being held from July to august 1979. The military handed over power to a civilian government on the 1st of October 1979.

At a dramatic ceremony at the Tafawa Balewa Square, Lagos, General Obasanjo stepped down for Alhaji Shehu Aliyu Shagari, who was then sworn in as the first Executive President of Nigeria. The ex-Head of State, General Obasanjo, and all the military officers who held political appointments during the military regime voluntarily retired from the Army with effect from the 1st of October 1979.

3

Peter Ofondu's father was being driven past Louis Mbanefo Street in Owerri to attend the christening of his grandson one Sunday when his car was caught in crossfire between feuding 'firms' of 4-1-9 which had a very strong presence in the Owerri Sector and were rumoured to have underpinned the functioning of the recently opened Owerri Airport. With their headquarters reputedly in Lagos, the 4-1-9 syndicates were said to have contacts in high places, including the police, the military, the judiciary, and even the Central Bank of Nigeria.

They were heavily involved in expatriate

contract shams using forged papers, or even

genuine fronts. Armed robbery, protection

rackets, prostitution rings, property frauds,

public and clandestine executions, all came

readily within their remit. Wherever they

operated, there was gruesome terror and

insecurity. In fact, the Abacha regime became

synonymous with all that 4-1-9 stood for.

Godwin Diya was a bear of a man, of

powerful physique and compelling personality.

He could dominate any situation or

conversation, and often did. It is easy to

visualize the figure he cut in the criminal culture

of 4-1-9. He was an ex-soldier and had served

prison sentences for all manner of offences,

including armed robbery for which he was

nearly shot. His resentments were reinforced, not resolved, by the various sentences, the desire to retaliate burnt even deeper into him. The seeds of his future adult criminality were nurtured and nourished when as a youngster he witnessed the gang-rape of his mother by armed robbers, who then beat him into unconsciousness. The lesson and the philosophy of life he was left with was that might is right, the harder you're hit, the harder you hit back. Godwin Diya eventually became the feared powerful leader of the main 4-1-9 'firm' in Owerri, assisted by his half-brother Abia.

Godwin Diya's first brush with the authorities was at the age of 14 when he badly beat up his headmaster at school and threatened

to carve up his face with his pen knife; he swore
that he was unfairly failed in his school
examinations. He was taken in a van to a
purpose-built detention centre near Enugu, for
up to 50 hard-nosed thugs. To a 14-year-old it
seemed like the end of the world. If he felt
lonely being driven through the thick steel gates
and across a huge compound surrounded by
very high barbed-wire fencing, it was nothing to
the frightening isolation he would experience in
the next 48 hours. He strutted cockily into the
reception area, in the middle of the compound,
his mind racing with what he would have to do
to make his stay as bearable as possible.

Someone, he was sure, would mark his
card, tell him who was there, what was going
on, advise him on what scams he could get into.

Not so. He just walked into a deafening

wall of silence. It was the first time he had seen

a prison officer and there were about four of

them, all glaring at him as if he was some dead

bird or mouse the dog had brought in. He started

to ask a question. It was the worst thing he

could have done.

'Shut your filthy mouth!' one of them

bawled in a heavy deadpan tone. 'We don't

want to hear from you, you nasty piece of

work.'

'Who the bollocks are you talking to?'

Godwin Diya shouted back. 'I'm –'

He never finished the sentence. The

prison officer threw himself at him and knocked

him over. They wrestled fanatically on the

ground, and the other prison officers pulled

them apart and dragged Godwin off the punishment block. They locked him in a bare concrete cell just over five and a half feet square.

Some four hours later someone brought Godwin some food, *okara*-balls and *moi-moi*. He had hardly had time to finish these when he was told to strip and change into the detention center uniform, which included boots he could hardly squeeze into. Then, a rough bed and some threadbare red blankets were brought in by two officers, who didn't say a word, either to each other or to Godwin. He found sleep hard, but finally dropped off in the early hours of the morning.

At six o'clock, Godwin's cell door opened and he was brought out of deep slumber by someone yelling, 'Get out of bed right away!' Godwin squinted through sleepy eyes at the door: two large screws built like iroko trees were standing there.

'Get out of that bed!'

He clambered out and stood up, in just his shorts. They frog-marched him out of his cell and forced him out on to the parade ground to do rapid press-ups to order, as well as bunny-hopping around in circles carrying heavy logs. Other inmates had joined him.

'Right you nasty little bastards, thugs and gangsters. I'll learn you a thing or two.'

The most menacing of the screws glared at them, each one in turn. Then his lip curled contemptuously.

'I'm going to make you very, very strong. By the time I've finished with you, you'll be the strongest thugs who ever walked this earth. I will give you the strongest coshing and battling arm in the business.'

He paused. His eyes ran over them all again. 'Now pick up your logs and start hopping. Hop, hop, hop, hop. Faster… faster… faster… faster.'

They were left gasping, but were still forced to bunny hop in groups of three to the showers. Carrying their logs, of course. Some of the punishments meted out were vicious and cruel. Though most of the grueling tasks they were given were pointless, many were useful and kept their youthful energy under control.

4

Peter Ofondu left Lagos Murtala Muhammed International airport and tried for a connecting local flight. He soon discovered that flights to Owerri airport were a lottery now the activities of 4-1-9 in the area had come under judicial scrutiny and investigation at long last. He decided instead to fly to Port Harcourt and then get home to Owerri by road.

There was a spectacular and undignified bus-stop-like scramble to get on board the last private airline (Okada) flight to Port Harcourt for the day. Peter gave generous *dashes* to several intermediaries to get on that flight, which was crowded with mostly Shell oil-operatives, some with their families, returning to their posts in Port Harcourt. It soon began to pour with rain and most of the passenger got badly soaked dashing from uncomfortable internal airport buildings across the wet tarmac to the plane. They then sat on the plane for an hour because of 'technical difficulties' before take-off. The expatriate pilot apologized for the delay. The Cyrillic script inside the plane suggested that the plane was probably made in one of the erstwhile Soviet Bloc countries.

It was evening and nightfall came suddenly. What a scenic sight once they were aloft and cruising towards Port Harcourt and Ogoni-land! The spectacular rain forests were candle-lit by multiple flares from the burning Niger Delta oil-well gases.

Arrival at Port Harcourt was a bit of an anti-climax. It was dark and wet and somewhat humid. The Shell oil-workers were comfortably sorted with laid-on transport from their company. For the rest of the passengers only a few taxis were available, and they were charging exorbitant prices, perhaps three times the expected rate, on a take-it-or-leave-it-basis. Peter got into one of the taxis en route to Owerri. He began to sympathize with the taxi driver and all road users in general in the area, as soon as they had done the first few miles.

Despite Nigeria being one of the major world oil producers especially in the delta area around Port Harcourt (Ogoni-land), petrol and other fuels were in desperately short supply and wickedly expensive, often five to ten times the 'official' price. It was not unusual for vehicles of all types to be parked around petrol stations for days, awaiting new fuel supplies. The roads, especially in old Biafra, were sadly neglected – and dangerous. With any heavy downpour, the countless and often large potholes became ensnaring mini-lakes where vehicles often stalled, and these vehicles, large and small, would zig-zag around the mini-lakes, often on a collision course.

Fuel was apparently being imported into the country by General Abacha's cronies! The basic infrastructures were crumbling away. Vehicle parts were increasingly difficult to find and the roadworthiness of most vehicles that managed to run was often a joke. The

educational and health sectors also seemed in

shambles and those employed in them were not

paid for several months.

A bag of cement, already high at 500

naira, had suddenly shot up to 1000 naira. The

local economy, despite the amazing ingenuity

and improvisations of the people, was beginning

to stall. The cost of basic foodstuffs was

becoming increasingly out of reach for the

ordinary Nigerian.

Meanwhile the reputed $12.2 billion

Gulf War windfall published by an official

enquiry had remained missing from the regime

of former military strongman General Ibrahim

Babangida. It was he who annulled the

presidential election of 1993, denying victory to

Abiola. This ushered Nigeria, Africa's most populous nation, into a five-year nightmare under his former second-in-command, General Sani Abacha, who apparently seized power to wrong-foot the restless Young Turks in the military opposed to the evil genius of Babangida.

Abacha had pre-emptively publicly declared himself, earlier on, a champion of the return to democratically elected government, with the army back in barracks!

5

Ben Kanu was a radical journalist and a campaigning editor of a national weekly at odds with the Abacha regime. He came from a rich well-respected family in Mbieri, near Owerri. One of his brothers was a specialist surgeon, another an architect, and a third a diplomat. His father was an *ozo* – a traditional Chief.

In the twilight months of General Abacha he was detained and tortured for his persistent opposition to the General's plans for change. He was released from detention by General Abubakar when he took over as his military Head of State following the death of

Abacha.

At that time, the military government

and those who wanted Abacha to continue to

rule beyond 1998 were not best pleased with

Ben Kanu. He believed he was just making his

comments innocently in weeklies and foreign

radio stations. However, the security operatives

(SSS) were angry with him over the interviews

he granted the BBC and, especially, the Voice

of America. They replayed that interview to him

at the headquarters of the SSS in Abuja on the

first day of his arrest. To effect his arrest, they

just sent somebody to his house, saying that

their director in Imo State wanted to see him.

When he got to Owerri, they said that they were

waiting for a plane to take him to Abuja.

He was given a room in Abuja in the morning. Some officials of the SSS took him to an office to get a statement from him.

'Why do you dislike the government and Abacha?'

'I do not dislike Abacha or his government.' Ben Kanu replied. 'I only want the best for our country.'

They then started to show him that they had damming evidence that he was trying to destabilize the country and that he was mobilizing people to achieve his aim. Ben Kanu made a 50-page statement stressing that those who wanted to destabilize Nigeria were the advisers of the Head of State.

Ben Kanu continued: 'All I do is just exercise my rights of speech as a citizen of this country. My views are the same as those of the majority of Nigerians, except, of course, those people in government who benefit from the unfortunate situation we find ourselves in.'

On the fifth day of his detention, around two o'clock in the morning, about ten gangster bruisers came in through the office where his statement had been taken. They just came and opened his door. One of them said his attention was needed. Four more of them were sitting in the office. Ben Kanu walked in saying, 'Peace be unto you,' but he couldn't remember whether they answered him.

'What's your name?' one of them screamed.

Immediately after, one of the gang began to flog him with a whip while another sprayed tear-gas in his face. They then put his hands

behind him and hand-cuffed him.

'Why don't you like Abacha? Why are

you opposed to his staying on in office?'

'I don't hate Abacha. Even Abacha has

not said that he will continue in office.'

Ben Kanu then stated his reasons for not

wanting Abacha to stay on in power. He said

there was no light, no fuel and no potable

drinking water in the country. He told them that

most of Abacha's ministers were criminals,

some of them had been convicted and that they

continued to steal, yet Abacha did not do

anything to them. And he couldn't pretend not

to know that they were misappropriating the

nation's money.

They were evidently very displeased about an interview Ben Kanu had granted VOA in which he said that General Abacha was not a politician and would not be one because he didn't interact with people. He had added that General Abacha contrived to lock himself up in Aso Rock like a woman in purdah and did not even go to mosque.

After brutally beating him up yet again, they came back the next day, begging him to join them to work for Abacha.

Ben Kanu protested to the Director of SSS in Abuja over his humiliation while in custody, but the SSS Director earnestly denied sending the thugs to him. They were indeed shocked at the state of his puffed-up and bruised eyes and face, so Ben Kanu suspected that the

thugs came from Aso Rock, the military rulers'
and Abacha's fortress headquarters in Abuja.

He recalled having dreams in detention
about the likelihood of Abacha being removed
from power, but it was all rather ill-defined. At
the SSS headquarters there was no
communication whatsoever. The place was
comfortable, with the air conditioners, but the
SSS never spoke to him. None of the SSS
operatives even disclosed their names. They
only came to Ben Kanu to give him food.

He did not know about Abacha's death.
It was only after he had been released and was
on his way back home that he saw a magazine
which carried the story. He guessed there and
then that Abacha's death had caused his release.
Only God knew, he reflected, what could have

happened to him under such an evil and reckless

regime.

6

Godwin Diya grew up fast in the ways of the world. He resolved to find or do something that would get some serious money. He wanted to have the nice things of life, and he was keen to do something impressive, with a touch of style.

He arrived at Port Harcourt and trouble did not take long to find him there. As he and his latest girlfriend, Beatrice, were walking to a food-parlour near the bus station, a group of youngsters called out suggestive comments to Beatrice. He ran towards them, and they scarpered, but he chased one of them and cornered him at the back of the food-parlour. He

pulled out a knife, intending to teach him a

lesson he'd never forget, but suddenly thought it

wasn't worth it, and gave him a sharp dig

instead.

After some careful thinking, Godwin

Diya came to the conclusion that the smartest

way to make his serious money was by safe

breaking, in partnership with his half-brother

Abia who adored him and looked up to him as

'big brother'. They targeted the African

Continental Bank and the First Bank of Nigeria.

A couple of weeks later, Godwin Diya

and Abia blew a safe of the First Bank of

Nigeria near Port Harcourt harbor and pulled

out 10,000 naira – serious money indeed. They

had help from men in the gelignite business who

also had their share of the loot. They did a

couple more jobs but with much less success.

Godwin Diya now felt he had money in

his pocket, twinned with a very raunchy passion

in his heart, He had gone to a night club in the

late hours of the night seen a feisty, glamorous

young woman at the bar – a waitress with a

rather revealing low-cut dress, taunting looks,

long lovely legs, well-endowed bust and behind,

and provocative movements. They got talking,

more by luck than by any skilled planning on

his part. But he failed to pull her.

An hour later, he was standing on a

corner, looking for a taxi, when he heard raised

voices. He saw the waitress, whose name he had

learned was Joy, having an argument with a

rough-looking fellow, who, it turned out, had

followed her from the club and was trying to persuade her to go somewhere with him.

When Godwin Diya asked the chap if he knew Joy, he told him to push off, because it was none of his business.

'This lady doesn't want to know you,' Godwin said. 'If you don't get going now, I'm going to splatter you over the pavement.'

'You splatter met?' he said.

'That's right, thickhead,' Godwin told him. 'Now make yourself scarce.'

'I want this woman,' he said.

'This woman does not want you,' Godwin said. 'She was waiting here for me.'

The buffer wouldn't have it, so Godwin gave him a powerful left-hander, then a right-hander that sent him sprawling and puffing.

Godwin then stopped a passing taxi and told the

driver to take them to where Joy said she lived.

When they got there, Godwin still

believed that there was nothing vulnerable or

soft about Joy. She seemed brazen, and quite

full of herself to the point of appearing arrogant.

Godwin was defensive, expecting a disagreeable

gold-digging girl-about-town. But he got a

shock: she was less forceful, much softer, and

physically far more attractive than when he first

became aware of her at the night club. So they

started chatting generally, and discovered that

their instincts were not too dissimilar and that

they liked each other.

She first thanked him softly for coming

to her rescue.

'But I can look after myself, you know,' she added, with a mischievous twinkle in her eyes.

Godwin was already enchanted by her and was surprisingly too frightened to touch her. But she made the first move and came up close to him; his head seemed to reel from the fragrance of her perfume. She bent over in front of Godwin and her breasts drifted neatly free from the cleavage of her dress. She fixed her probing gaze on him and sat on his lap. She slipped her dress off her shoulders and in one deft move her knickers were on the floor. She then turned her back on him, and turned round slowly, completely naked, to face him. She brushed her impressively firm breasts against his face and nose, pulled off his trousers and boxer shorts, and threw away his shirt. He

hardened instantly and they did it, many times

over.

Half an hour later, she dismissed him,

and said, 'See you sometime, lover-boy.'

7

Godwin Diya and his half-brother Abia were in great form one Friday night, laughing and joking in a seedy hotel after pulling off a spectacular safe blowing in Owerri town centre near the Ikenga Statue roundabout. It was a senior 4-1-9 member's birthday, and they were throwing a party: a typical 4-1-9 knees-up with scantily clad prostitutes, most of them forced into service by the 4-1-9 terror squad. Senior members of the Owerri 4-1-9 firm were there, suited and booted, all drinking, with smiles on their hard faces. High-life music was thumping.

The wives and girlfriends were there too, all dolled up and smelling nice.

The 4-1-9 gang owned the hotel, as well as lots of property and other interests in the state, some compulsorily acquired on pain of being maimed horribly or bumped off, often without ceremony. A well-known and respected local doctor who had trained in the United States had just returned home after the death of his father at a private hospital in Owerri. He was confronted by the 4-1-9 gang, who demanded an exorbitant ransom for the release of his father's body for burial. The distraught doctor would have none of it.

The next day, members of the gang abducted his 11-year-old daughter from school and she was never seen again. For months he pleaded with the police authorities for help and got nowhere.

At the party, Godwin Diya and his half-brother Abia were lapping it up. Most of the gang had tossed large-denomination naira notes into a big calabash bowl on the bar, and the palm wine, star beer and other drinks kept flowing non-stop. Amphetamines and other illegal drugs also abounded.

Behind all the jollity, Godwin Diya and Abia had orchestrated a ruthless plan to eliminate a rival 4-1-9 gang leader in Owerri. Louis Mbanefo Street in Owerri was the gangland's discreet centre of operations. The rival gang leader, Everest Dada, was a hunky, ruthless loner, always in dark glasses, who liked nothing better than to get drunk and bed women, the younger the sweeter. But when he got involved in selling amphetamines and other illegal drugs and started taking them himself, he lost his common sense and started challenging Godwin Diya and his brother. To them he had become a nuisance that had to be eliminated.

They invited him to the party via a neutral 4-1-9 gang member, Joe Iyam.

'There's a party going on,' Joe Iyam said to Everest Dada. 'Plenty of young birds and all the rest of it. Let's go there.'

'Why not,' Everest Dada replied.

They got into Everest Dada's new sleek Buick saloon. Everest Dada was driving. He was laughing and joking; he couldn't wait to get to the party.

He parked in a side street opposite where the party was being held and they strolled across. They took a back entrance and walked up half-a-dozen steps and knocked on the door. It was opened by a pretty scantily clad young woman and Everest Dad's spirits swelled. She led them along a narrow corridor and down some stairs.

Everest Dada was first, still eager to get to the party, followed by Joe Iyam. There was a basement room leading from the stairs. Everest Dad strolled in there laughing. 'Where are the girls and where's the party, then? Everest is here!'

But there was to be no party for Everest, only a trap. Seconds after he walked into that room, Godwin Diya half ran towards him and put a gun to the back of his head. He pulled the

trigger on Everest. But the gun failed to fire. He

pulled it again and Everest Dada slumped to the

floor, his brains splattered on the walls and

floor.

8

The case of the doctor and his abducted

11-year-old daughter so affected the local

population that the 4-1-9 gang were taken aback

when a spontaneous violent backlash against

them erupted. Their mansions and other ill-

gotten property that could be identified were set

alight.

The local population were no longer

afraid of their threats. Vigilante groups

emerged, organized by Peter Ofondu. He

employed his past military experience to sniff

out the leaders of the gang and their hideouts.

He helped stiffen the resolve of the judicial,

military and police authorities to crack down on the 4-1-9 mafia.

One morning the phone rang at Joe Iyam's house. It was Beatrice, Godwin Diya's girlfriend.

'Have you heard the news?'

'What news?' Joe Iyam asked.

'About Godwin Diya and Abia,' she said. 'They've been nicked.'

It did not take Joe Iyam long to find out what had happened. The local newspapers and radio and television news bulletins were full of the dramatic dawn swoop by a large combined armed police and military force to capture Godwin Diya. His half-brother Abia and the senior members of their firm. They were going to be charged, it seemed, under the Advanced

Fee Fraud Criminal Code Section 419.

The next day Joe Iyam was pulled in

himself. He was staying at a hotel, and was

woken early in the morning by armed police

breaking down the bedroom door while he was

having it off with one of the young female

prostitutes of the gang. They gave him just

enough time to get dressed before whisking him

off to the heavily guarded incident centre at

Owerri. The man put in charge of the operation,

Chief Superintendent Stephen Osita, had been

specially drafted from the Enugu CID.

He told Joe Iyam that they knew that he

had 'some knowledge' of a murder. If he co-

operated, they would make it worth his while.

'I don't know what you're talking about,' he protested. 'I have had a drink with Godwin Diya, but that's as far as it goes. I wasn't at any party. I don't even remember going to any party with someone named Everest Dada.'

Stephen Osita looked at him piercingly. 'Are you absolutely sure?'

'One hundred and one percent,' he said. 'I wouldn't have anything to do with anything like that.'

Deep inside, though, Joe Iyam was less assured and indeed was shell-shocked, someone had obviously made a statement. But he was not going to incriminate himself.

Chief Superintendent Stephen Osita nodded his head gravely. 'I don't believe you.

I'm not pussy-footing, Joe Iyam. Co-operate –

or else…' he thundered.

He took Joe Iyam down to the police

morgue, where some of the victims of recent 4-

1-9 gangland fights were unveiled.

'Co-operate with us or we can arrange

for you to end up as one of these,' Chief

Superintendent Stephen Osita pressed home his

onslaught.

Iyam's bottle went. They were deadly

serious. He knew they would do it – even that

night. Chief Superintendent Stephen Osita was

now furious. He told someone to take Joe Iyam

to a room and leave him there to think things

over. A couple of hours later, Joe Iyam was

brought back before the Chief Superintendent

again and he resumed grilling him with more

questions, looking never more menacing.

Throughout the morning and afternoon

the Chief Superintendent kept questioning him,

then leaving him on his own. Joe Iyam was

knackered and drained. He hadn't had any sleep

for more than 28 hours. His brain was racing,

like a computer looking for all the angles. He

wanted to tell the truth: he was at least an

accessory to the murder of Everest Dada. But he

feared revenge from the 4-1-9 operatives.

Towards the evening, Chief

Superintendent Stephen Osita's patience ran out

and he snapped. He took a heavy rubber police

truncheon, ran across the room, and whacked

Joe Iyam round the back with it. It convinced

Joe Iyam, if it had not sunk in already, that he was in trouble. Big, big trouble.

He was locked in a small brick cell. There was no bed, only a dirty raffia mat. He was left alone in that cell for 11 hours. It was the loneliest time of his life. Finally, exhaustion overpowered him. He stretched his long bulky frame on the disgusting strip of raffia mat and closed his eyes. He had not slept for 48 hours.

9

The next day Joe Iyam was very co-operative and told all, grassing on Godwin Diya and his firm.

Two weeks later, at the Central Criminal Court in Owerri, Godwin Diya, his half-brother Abia and most of their firm and other leaders of the 4-1-9 gang stood together in the dock as the charges were read out: 'You are charged that on such-and-such a date at such-and-such an address etc., you did, with others, murder, extort, abduct, maim…'

Bail was refused and they were all remanded in custody. As the committal hearing went on, it was no longer a tiny newspaper paragraph or two. It whetted the public's appetite for sensational revenge on those who had terrorized and cowed them with such impunity for so long. It was a drama everyone, it was clear, wanted to see.

Queues for the public gallery formed every day, long before the accused arrived. It was edge-of-the-seat stuff. No one knew what to expect. Anything was possible. The 4-1-9 gang had very powerful friends in high places, even in the judiciary.

As the hearing went on, the police cannily played psychological games. They allowed all sorts of disquieting rumours to come into the prisoners' cells to feed their paranoia about who was, and who was not, going to go

against them.

Peter Ofondu was determined to avenge

the casual killing of his adored father by the 4-

1-9 gang. He saw to it that the judge in charge

of the proceedings was not bent. It was Mr.

Justice Edward Asika, 'The Hammer', as he was

known by the criminal underworld. He was

ruthless in his dispensation of Draconian

sentences when they appeared before him.

Secretly the criminal underworld respected his

integrity and fairness but that did not stop them

issuing several death threats to him, which he

disdainfully ignored.

The judge came into his own during the

summing-up when the moment arrived. He

ensured his place in Nigerian legal history in his

resumé of the court's grimmest and longest trial, which left the jury in no doubt there was only one possible verdict: guilty.

A chill ran through all the accused. The judge had laid it on the line. For the past ten weeks, the accused had climbed the steps from the cells together. Now they would go up one by one to be sentenced.

Godwin Diya was the first to be called. He was back in less than six minutes, His half-brother Abia was next, and was back even more quickly. And so on till all 13 of them had climbed the steps and back.

'GUILTY!'

They were to be sentenced the next day. The prosecution had demanded the death penalty by public military firing squad for their frightening and grisly catalogue of murders,

mayhem, extortion, prostitution rings,

abductions, drug cartels, money laundering, and

much else besides.

10

Chief Superintendent Stephen Osita had his rouges gallery of 4-1-9 members on his work desk. Those currently arraigned at the Central Criminal Court in Owerri were merely the tip of the iceberg of a sophisticated criminal organisation.

For first and foremost these guys were businessmen. Besides, the competing 'chapters' each had their own code of conduct and even mode of transport. Now and again, one by one, Stephen Osita would tap his pen on their photos.

'God forgives but 4-1-9 members don't...'

'And no prisoners taken…'

'Open season! Open season…!'

These were some of the slogans bandied about amongst them. The 4-1-9 syndicate had 'Bikers', 'Privateers', 'Sailors', 'Stranglers', 'Knifers', 'hangers', 'Rape-Gangers', 'Poisoners', 'Bombers'…

Chief Superintendent Stephen Osita was quite a character himself. He was tall and thin, almost skeletal. His brown eyes were slow-moving, deliberate, penetrating. He often wore a khaki-brown, sharply tailored 'Chinese' shirt buttoned up to the throat with no tie, and stovepipe trousers so narrow that the bones of his knees bulged through the material. His shoes were pointed in the Italian style and of grey suede. He chain-smoked. He was a frightening lizard of a man and criminals' skin crawled with fear of him.

He had served in an elite Biafran commando unit that spearheaded the attack and capture of Benin during the Biafran war. As a child he was pugnacious and self-assertive. He would hop about in a fury if he was denied, but soon afterwards he could laugh at himself.

His nerves and emotions were close to the surface, and he was tiresomely quick-tempered. The thwarting of any whim could mean tears and abuse. At school he was tediously argumentative and crudely personal in his comments, and this made him unpopular. But he was intellectually more mature than the other boys and sexually precocious; he lost his virginity at the age of 15 and had a way with local girls.

The loss of his parents in his early teens from a freak lightning strike in a thunderstorm seemed to have pushed him to develop marked self-sufficiency and assurance at an early age. He disliked the conventional views of things, often merely because they were conventional.

He was restless and unsettled after the end of the Biafran war in 1970. He wanted to be 'on the march again'. He was an unrepentant Ndigbo activist in the renewed call for a proper assessment of the position of the Igboman in Nigeria.

'We are fed up with bemoaning our dwindling fortunes since Abacha came to power. We must return to the mainstream of

Nigerian politics. But I must tackle and ablate

this cancerous 4-1-9 business first and foremost,

by fair means or foul…' he thought.

Stephen Osita felt that the Igbo were

right in demanding that they put in the scheme

of things, that it was high time their citizenship,

residency and minority rights were respected.

The Igbo, he felt, were still on the periphery

when it came to deciding who gets what, where,

and when in Nigeria.

He knew in his bones that the Igboman

was a determined businessman who knew what

he wanted, went after it and got it. As an ethnic

group in Nigeria today, the Igbo were respected

for their industry, doggedness and sheer

presence.

In the commercial sector, Stephen Osita reasoned, the Igbo held sway as they were Nigeria's foremost chance of ever making a technological breakthrough… Yet, they had continuously lost out in the power politics of the Nigerian nation. Could they be merely crying wolf? Was it possible for a people with so much determination and presence to be marginalized?

Almost all the markets in the North were controlled by Ndigbo. Long-distance travel and much of the road haulage business had been cornered by the Igbo, and one could throw in the handful of banks in which Ndigbo held sway. But the issue of marginalization, Stephen Osita thought, was not about such matters. He was considering the relative access of the constituent ethnic groupings to state power. And in a country where whoever controlled central political power was god, the others were bound to suffer discrimination. No doubt about it, in developing economies the start was the principal source of wealth.

Under the present structure of things, Stephen Osita said to himself, real wealth could only flow from state power, and the present state under General Abacha was so centralized that only those who had a proper hold on power could hope to provide the basic comforts of life for their people…

'Today, the worst expressway in Nigeria is unquestionably the Enugu-Aba Expressway. I should know,' Stephen Osita vehemently asserted to a reporter from Lagos, doing a vox pop. 'That was my patch before I thankfully moved to Enugu. The stretch is a veritable death trap and continues to suffer total neglect. Compare this with the roads in the north generally, and other parts of the country beyond Igboland.'

To Stephen Osita there were other indications of neglect and marginalisation. Look at the membership of the topmost ruling military legislative body over the years and the composition of the Federal Executive Council, he thought. And Igboland had been facing terrible problems of massive land erosion to which the central government had not given adequate attention, although it had disbursed huge sums to aid moribund agricultural effort in other parts of the country, especially the north.

The issue of marginalisation, Stephen Osita ruminated, was really that of how state-controlled resources were dispensed. Why should Igbo feel committed to the Nigerian project if, 30 years after the civil war, the process of re-integration had not made any noticeable impact on their re-integration had not made any noticeable impact on their ability to influence the dispensation of the collectively-owned resources; crude oil in particular, initially found and explored in their backyard, so to speak...

Or were the Igbo still being made to pay for the perceived sins of Biafra?

A detailed look at the statistics spanning the armed forces, the civil service, parastatals, security service and general federal presence, painted a picture of Igbo marginalisation in cold, startling colours… Maybe the Igbo were their own worst enemy – their so-called leaders having tended to prop up the most unpopular regimes the country had experienced?

Stephen Osita believed that a people as industrious as the Igbo would simply not be willing to do dirty jobs collectively as a people. They might, however, be deluded into thinking that these errand-boys were their leaders, representing their interests in Abuja, whereas this was not so.

'We cannot justify marginalization on the basis of the selfish collaboration of a few misguided elements…' he told himself. That was not the fundamental issue.

The marginalization of the Igbo was no worse than the marginalization of the Ogoni people or even to some extent that of the Yoruba and other neglected minority ethnic groupings in the Nigerian state. The crucial thing was what made marginalization impossible or unnecessary.

Yes, Stephen Osita was convinced marginalization was a structural problem pervading the consciousness of both the oppressor and the oppressed the former seeing it as God-given while the latter accepted it as inevitable. Igbo marginalization was merely a reflection of the marginalization of almost 50 other ethnic groupings in Nigeria. Though past governments had tried to downplay the marinization question, it was now becoming too

glaring to ignore.

The Igbo feel themselves special victims

and want to fight back as a nation!' he

concluded.

11

Donatus Eze was thinking about his light-skinned beautiful wife, Patience. For nearly two years he had deliberately tried to put the thought of her out of his mind. He hadn't wanted to remember.

It was too painful – too horrible. The blue cyanosed face, the convulsed clutching fingers… the contrast between that and the gay lovely Patience the day before her death… Of what good was remembrance? Forget it all! Forget the whole horrible business.

But now, he realized, he had got to remember. He had got to think back into the past, to remember carefully even slight, unimportant-seeming incidents. That extraordinary interview with Chief Superintendent Stephen Osita necessitated remembrance.

It had been so unexpected, so frightening.

Donatus Eze felt he had got to think about Patience – to remember Patience, his young bride. She had won a beauty contest. Donatus was there. He had fallen hopelessly in love with her.

'What a *beautiful* bride she will make,' he had thought feverishly.

Donatus Eze was well-off. He was 15 years older than Patience, and kindly, pleasant, but definitely dull. On the other hand Patience moved with frightening elegance, was soft-

voiced, graceful, with a swaying undulating

figure and big light brown eyes. A disturbingly

beautiful creature.

Donatus could not believe his good

fortune when, months later, after proposing on

his bended knees, she accepted his offer of

marriage.

For Patience there was excitement:

shopping, streams of parcels, bridesmaids,

dresses…

What Donatus Eze did not know was

that Patience had her own money, a great deal of

it. Her favourite Uncle Ezekiel's money. He had

made his fortune as an illegal wine merchant

importing huge amounts at rock bottom prices

from the Spanish island of Fernando Po just off

the Bight of Biafra.

Ezekiel Banjo wasn't really an uncle,

Patience had always known that. Without ever

having been told, she knew certain facts.

Ezekiel had been in love with her

equally beautiful mother Josephine. She had

preferred another and a poorer man. Ezekiel had

taken his defeat in a romantic spirit. He had

remained the family friend and adopted an

attitude of romantic platonic devotion. He had

become Uncle Ezekiel, had stood godfather

when Patience was born, and made it possible

for her to attend an expensive boarding school.

When he died of cirrhosis of the liver it was

found that he had left the bulk of his fortune to

his goddaughter.

Patience had a cousin, June, who did not believe Patience was ever really in love with Donatus. But she had seemed very happy with him and she had been fond of him. June had good opportunities for knowing, for a year after the marriage she was orphaned and Patience invited her, a shy girl of 16, to live with them.

A girl of 16… June pondered over the picture of herself. What had she felt, thought, seen?

June had accepted life as it came, had duly mourned for her parents. She had gone to live with Patience and her rich husband in their comfortable two-storey country house in Obazu-Mbieri.

Sometimes it had been rather dull in that house.

There were times when she had nothing much to do and nobody to talk to. Ezekiel was kind, invariably affectionate and avuncular. His attitude had never varied.

And Patience? June saw very little of Patience. Patience was out a great deal. Dressmakers, parties, beauty contests…

What did she *know* about Patience, when she came to think of it? Of her tastes, of her hopes, of her fears? Frightening, really, she thought, how little you might *know* of a person after living in the same house with them! There had been little or no intimacy between the cousins.

Certainly Patience had *seemed* happy enough. Until that day – when it happened.

Donatus too would never forget that day.

It stood out crystal clear – each detail. Donatus

closed his eyes and let the scene come back…

It was a sunny afternoon. He and

Patience were having lunch on the verandah. A

Toyota pick-up truck raced up their drive and

three men wearing balaclavas jumped out and

grabbed them by the throat.

'Gangers! 4-1-9… Gangers! 4-1-9,' they

growled.

Patience and Donatus were quickly tied

up and gagged. They ransacked their house and

took whatever money and valuables they could

lay their hands on.

Then they made Donatus watch as they

gang-raped Patience and strung her up on a tree,

still gagged, with her print dress. Donatus

watched her slowly die. He passed out.

The 'gangers' jumped back into their

truck with their loot and sped away.

12

Chief Superintendent Stephen Osita

listened carefully to Donatus Eze's account of

how Patience met her death.

'I'll get those scoundrels!' he said

gravely under his breath. 'I'll break their

scoundrel necks!'

June tried her best to console Donatus

after the death of Patience. She had continued to

live at their house. One day she decided to try

on a pretty dress which Patience had given her

just before her death. The dress had big pockets.

June shook the dress out, noting that it

was in perfectly good condition. Her hand felt

something crackle in one of the pockets. She

thrust in her hand and drew out a crumpled-up

piece of paper. It was in Patience's handwriting,

and she smoothed it out to read it.

Darling Festus… I am sorry about
Donatus – he's always been rather sweet
to me – but he'll understand. God meant
us for each other. I know He did. I shall
tell Donatus myself after one of our

lunches on the verandah… Festus darling.
I can't live without you… Just can't, can't
– CAN'T.

The letter broke off.

June stood motionless, staring down at

it.

How little one knew of one's own cousin! So Patience had had a lover – had written him passionate love letters – had planned to go away with him?

Who was this Festus? Did he love Patience as much as she loved him? Surely he must have done. Patience was so unbelievably lovely. Perhaps for him it had been a mere passing distraction. Perhaps he had never really cared.

Hadn't Patient been going to count the cost? She had seemed determined, though. June shivered. And she, June, hadn't known a thing about it! Hadn't even guessed.

She had taken it for granted that Patience was happy and contented and that she and Donatus were quite satisfied with one another.

Blind! She must have been blind not to know a thing like that about her own cousin.

Again, she asked herself, who was this Festus?

She cast her mind back, thinking, remembering.

There had been so many men about, admiring Patience, taking her out, ringing her up. She could not recall anyone special.

But there must have been – the rest of the bunch were mere camouflage for the one, the only one, that mattered. June frowned perplexedly, sorting her remembrances carefully.

Oh yes, Festus Ibeh. What could Patience have seen in him? A stiff, pompous young man – and not so very young either. Of course people did say he was doing brilliantly at the University of Nigeria, Enugu campus, and thought himself a future President. Was that what had given him glamour in Patience's eyes?

Surely she couldn't care so desperately for the man himself – such a cold, self-contained creature?

But they said that his own wife was passionately in love with him, that she had gone against all the wishes of her tribally powerful family in marrying him – a mere nobody with political ambitions!

Perhaps if one woman felt like that way about him, another woman might also. Odd the way Festus Ibeh had disappeared after Patience's death. No one had seen him since.

13

Even now, thinking back, June could not put her finger on the moment when it began. Ever since Patience's death Donatus had been abstracted, had had fits of inattention and brooding. He had seemed older, heavier.

That was all natural enough. But when exactly had his abstraction become something more than natural? It was, she thought, after she mentioned the name of Festus Ibeh that she had first noticed him staring at her in a bemused, perplexed manner.

Then he formed a new habit of coming home early from business and shutting himself up in his study. He didn't seem to be doing

anything there. She had gone in once and found

him sitting at his desk, staring straight ahead of

him. He looked at her when she came in with

dull, lacklustere eyes.

Donatus looked like a man who has had

a shock, but to her question as to what was the

matter, he replied, 'Nothing. Nothing at all.'

As the days went by, he went about with

the careworn look of a man who was battling

with several worries on his mind. Nobody had

paid very much attention. June certainly hadn't.

Worries were always conveniently 'business'.

Then at odd intervals, and with no

seeming reason, he began to ask questions. It

was then that June began to put his manner

down as definitely 'odd'.

'Tell me, June, did Patience ever talk to you much?'

June stared at him. 'Why, of course, Donatus. At least – well, about what?

'Oh, herself – her friends – how things were going with her. Whether she was happy or unhappy. That sort of thing.'

June thought she saw what was in his mind. He must have got wind of Patience's love affair.

She said slowly, 'She never said much. I mean, she was always busy – parties, doing things.'

'And you were only shy sweet sixteen. Yes, I know. All the same, I thought she might have said something.' He looked at her enquiringly – rather like a hopeful dog.

June did not want Donatus to be hurt. And anyway Patience never had said anything. She shook her head.

Donatus sighed. He said heavily, 'Oh well, it doesn't matter.'

Another day he asked her suddenly who Patience's best women friends had been.

June reflected. She reluctantly mentioned a couple of names.

'How intimate was she with them?'

'Well, I don't know exactly.'

'I mean, do you think she might have confided in any of them?'

I don't really know – I don't think it is very likely… What sort of confiding do you mean?'

Immediately she wished she hadn't asked that last question, but Donatus' response to it surprised her.

'Did Patience ever say she was afraid of anybody?'

'Afraid?' June started.

'What I'm trying to get at is, did Patience have any enemies?'

'Amongst other women?'

'No, no, not that kind of thing. Real enemies. Threats from 4-1-9 say, because of her known wealth and beauty. They might have had it in for her.'

June's scared stare seemed to upset him.

'Sounds silly, I know,' he muttered. 'Melodramatic perhaps, but I just wondered.'

June continued to stare. She looked like a sphinx now.

Donatus passed his hand over his forehead. 'You don't understand what I'm talking about. Don't look so scared, June. You've got to help me. You've got to remember every damned thing you can. Now, now, I know I sound a bit batty and incoherent, but you'll understand in a minute – when I've shown you this postcard I found in Patience's favorite handbag.'

He drew a red postcard from his hip pocket, with words printed on it in small zig-zag letters.

'Read that,' said Donatus.

June stared down at the postcard. What it said was quite clear and devoid of circumlocution: *4-1-9 CALLING! 4-1-9*

CALLING!

June shivered. She was frightened

now… horribly frightened.

14

The getaway pick-up Toyota van used by the 4-1-9 killers of Patience was involved in an accident. Peter Ofondu was driving down from Owerri to Mbieri when he became suspicious of the reckless driving of a pick-up van, redolent of the arrogance of the 4-1-9 operatives in the area who considered themselves above the law and kings of the road when 'on business.'

Word had spread quickly about the hanging of Patience.

Peter Ofondu was prepared for a confrontation with the operatives. He had five heavily armed vigilantes in his reinforced Ford

Transit van. They managed to force the pick-up

truck off the road near the entrance to a narrow

one-way wooden bridge across a stream. Peter

and his men rammed the truck, and the three 4-

1-9 operatives jumped off into the stream.

Peter's commando skills, learnt in the Biafran

special forces unit, began to emerge.

'Henry!' Peter Ofondu shouted to one of

the vigilantes. 'I'll go after them. Check their

pick-up truck and retrieve whatever you can.'

'No problem, sir.'

A shot from one of the 4-1-9 men grazed

Peter's left should. Peter fired back and hit one

of them fatally in the forehead, Peter then

jumped into the stream, overpowered a second

4-1-9 member and drowned him in seconds,

after dealing him a karate chop. The third member of the gang fled into the nearby bush.

The other vigilantes gave chase. The surviving 4-1-9 operative was running hell for leather across the wet grass by the stream. The light rain was letting up, but that grass was soaking and slippery under Peter's hopeless flat soles, and he knew he wasn't making enough speed.

'Hold it, or you're dead meat!' the 4-1-9 operative shouted at the chasing vigilantes as he suddenly stopped and took aim. He dispatched one of the vigilantes, Zak, with cool, practiced ease. The others fell back and melted into a nearby thicket.

Peter, however, pressed on, but a bit more cagily, weaving and diving. The shots still came, carefully, evenly spaced, and like bees

whipped annoyingly past Peter and slapped into

the grass. Peter dodged and zigzagged, his skin

quivering as he waited for the next bullet.

It was terrible going. Peter dived into a

thicket. Overlapping branches tore at the arms

he crossed over his face.

It began to get dark rather suddenly and

Peter couldn't see more than a few yards ahead.

There was little room for manoeuvre and he just

had to make headway in whatever direction the

thicket allowed him. His breath was sobbing out

of his throat. His clothes had begun to tear, and

he could feel bruises all over his body.

But why no bullets? Peter wondered. He

stumbled to his right and found a better cover

and dived to his knees among soaking leaves.

He waited for the rasping of his breath to quieten down.

And then Peter heard a noise as if someone was coming towards him, not softly but steadily, and stopping every now and then to listen. By now the 4-1-9 operative was well aware that from the silence that Peter was in hiding and had gone to ground.

If he knew anything about tracking, Peter reflected, he would soon find where the broken branches and scuffed earth stopped. Then it would only be a question of time. Peter softly squirmed round to the back of one of the bigger trees in the thicket.

The feet and the snapping twigs were coming nearer. Now he could hear some heavy breathing. Peter lay still, hardly breathing. He had set up a sort of twig trip wire close to where he was hiding.

His luck held.

The 4-1-9 operative stumbled ignominiously over the tripwire. Peter pounced and a fierce hand-to-hand struggle ensued. The 4-1-9 operative was slick and strong but Peter got the better of him and had him by the throat.

'Don't kill me,' he begged. 'You can have any amount of money you want… I have good connections with the Central Bank of Nigeria.'

Blood was oozing from a cut above the temple of his tough, sly-looking face. As Peter watched, the blood trickled down towards his chin. But disturbingly, his face remained unmoved… It showed no pain, only a terrifying

intensity of purpose.

Peter bound his wrists behind his back

and led him to his waiting Ford Transit van.

There he met up with the surviving vigilantes,

who had recovered the body of Zak, their mate

who had been shot by the 4-1-9 operative.

15

The captured 4-1-9 operative turned out

to be a very important person in the organization

when he was handed over to Chief

Superintendent Stephen Osita for interrogation.

'Your name?' Stephen Osita began.

'Christian.'

'What a travesty! Christian what?'

'Christian Ajemba.'

Chief Superintendent Stephen Osita was

not going to pussyfoot around. He opened one

of his drawers and pulled out a card with

someone's photograph and personal details on it.

'That's you,' he said.

Christian Ajemba pretended not to know what he was talking about. He looked at the card, then at Stephen Osita. 'No, it's not.'

'Oh yes, it is.'

'Really?'

'We have information from Lagos and Abuja,' Stephen Osita continued, 'that you, your wife and Chief Emmanuel Udeh are pushing stolen money through the international banking system.

Christian Ajemba's heart sank. What was going on here? He stared ahead, not taking in what was being said. It was as if Stephen Osita was talking to someone else.

He shook his head. He showed no emotion; it was not touching him. Chief Superintendent Osita was talking to a lump of flesh, not him. He was out of it, looking down the whole thing…

'Why am I here?' Christian Ajemba protested unconvincingly.

'For doing virgins out of season!' Stephen Osita replied sarcastically. 'Do you remember a Mr. Nelson Guchi, a Brazilian director of Banco Noroeste, based in Sao Paulo?'

'Who the hell is he?'

'Let me refresh your putrid mind. You and Chief Emmanuel Udeh were introduced to Mr. Nelson Guchi, posing convincingly as the governor and deputy governor of the Central

Bank of Nigeria, with your wife hanging around the wings. You tantalized Mr. Guchi with the promise of a share in a large fee paid to the bank in exchange for it providing funds to build a Nigerian airport contrary to the 4-1-9 Schedule of the Criminal Code against upfront fee fraud.'

Christian Ajemba was determined not to lose his bottle. But his brain was racing, like a computer, looking for all the angles.

He began to recall the events that began on a business trip to Nigeria in 1994 by the said Mr. Guchi. Despite the obvious scam, the Banco Noroeste director accepted the terms of the offer from them and returned to Sao Paulo, where he began to receive demands for taxes and other payments to procure the business. In all, through one of the bank's subsidiaries registered in the

Cayman Islands, Mr. Guchi paid out $190 million to a variety of companies in an effort to get his cut of the fee.

The supposed Central Bank of Nigeria demanded from Mr. Guchi various 'mandatory deposit taxes', 'fictional marginal charges' and 'statutory fees' – payments that would 'secure' the business.

The siphoning off of the money from the Cayman Islands bank account was not picked up by Banco Noroeste's own auditors Price Waterhouse Coopers, which issued unqualified certificates for the subsidiary for years.

The theft, which went on for three years, was noticed only in 1997 when Banco Santander Central Hispano, Spain's biggest bank, decided to purchase Banco Noroeste for

$500 million. The Spanish bank's own

accountants noticed a financial discrepancy at

the Cayman Islands operation and immediately

interviewed Mr. Guchi, who had almost sole

control of money being moved in and out of the

Cayman Island accounts.

Mr. Guchi, when questioned, claimed

that some money had gone to provide funding

for a Nigerian airport, more cash had gone on

speculative arbitrage in currencies, and other

sums had been paid to a Brazilian voodoo

princess.

Further enquiries uncovered losses of

$240 million, as money had been transferred

from the Cayman Islands subsidiary via New

York to accounts and banks around the world.

The investigation found that $40 million had found its way directly to the UK, of which $8 million was paid through the Docklands branch of Barclays under the very noses of the UK regulators.

According to the claim in the High court the Barclays account was held on behalf of a company called Macdaniels Limited, a business claiming to be a bureau de change registered in the UK whose director was Chief Ezugo Dan Nwandu – a business associate of Christian Ajemba. Ajemba used Chief Nwandu's foreign exchange facilities in Nigeria to handle money generated from Dax Petroleum, one of his companies.

Despite the fact that Macdaniels had a turnover of just £14,622 in 1997, the arrival of three large payments from Banco Noroeste's Cayman Operation (of $1,750,000 $2,750,000 and $3,550,000) did not raise any comment at Barclays. Nor were alarm bells triggered when cash was almost immediately transferred out of the account.

For instance, nearly $200,000 was paid to Quattro Jewelers for the provision of 'his and hers' diamond encrusted 18-carat gold Rolex watches for Ajemba and his wife.

A further $267,000 was used to purchase French period furniture which ended up being exported to Ajemba in Nigeria. Money was also transferred to Dax Petroleum and to other companies controlled by him. Barclays refused to comment on the case, saying it was a matter of confidentiality!

The pattern of the Macdaniels account was repeated in other jurisdictions around the world, with $126 million arriving in Swiss banks, $6.2 million in Hong Kong and $17.5 million in New York.

The scam took a sinister turn when Chief Emmanuel Udeh was killed in a road accident in Nigeria – the local press claimed he had been murdered by his 4-1-9 business partners.

The investigation into the trail of money finally came to a head when lawyers acting for the shareholders of the Brazilian bank issued orders freezing the assets of, among others, Macdaniels, Chief Nwandu, Dax Petroleum, and also the assets of Christian and his wife.

Those lawyers uncovered property assets in the UK worth around £5 million at locations in Regent's Park, Finchley, Golders Green and Hendon, all in North London.

Despite the enormity of the fraud, the tale had one last ironic twist. The suspicious death of Chief Emmanuel Udeh did not prevent tax returns in his name being provided to the UK's Inland Revenue, even though the Revenue was demanding inheritance tax on his estate!

The tax returns declared the rental income earned on his London property.

A chill ran through Christian Ajemba as he recalled a saying by Benjamin Franklin: 'But in this world nothing can be said certain, except death and taxes.'

16

Chief Superintendent Stephen Osita was shitting himself at what he had got, what a prize prey he had caught. But he felt rather disconcerted when he turned on his radio later that night and heard on the BBC World Service 'Plundered $1 billion to be returned to Nigeria.'

The report said the family of General Sani Abacha- the reputed 4-1-9 godfather and former Nigerian President who plundered more than $3 Billion of State cash in the 1990s – has agreed to return about $1 billion (£695 million) in an out-of-court settlement.

The agreement shunted one of the biggest international money-laundering cases towards an unexpected early close.

The Nigerian authorities had agreed to cancel all legal actions against Mohammed Abacha, the former President's son, his associates and member of the Abacha family who participated in the settlement, freeing them from the threat of multimillion dollar fines.

Only Abdulkadir Abacha, the former President's brother, remained on the list of potential defendants in connection with some $190 million he was alleged to have hidden in Switzerland.

Swiss banks, which held the bulk of General Abacha's plundered loot, would return $535 million to the Nigerian Government.

Banks in Jersey were expected to return some $200 million, and banks in Luxembourg and Liechtenstein a total of $300 million.

No money was apparently found in Britain although an investigation involving the Serious Fraud Office (SFO), the Metropolitan Police, the Home Office and the Financial Services Authority found traces of $1.3 billion which had passed though the City.

More than $100 million would be returned to the Abacha family by the banks in Switzerland because it could be proved that the money had been removed from the country before General Abacha came to power!

The settlement left more than $2 billion of Abacha's loot unaccounted for, with little prospect of its ever being recovered. The settlement came after the SFO and the Home Office helped to gather a huge body of evidence to support the Nigerian Government's legal action.

Chief Superintendent Stephen Osita muttered ruefully under his breath: 'When 4-1-9 greed takes over, how people and big money get laundered.'

17

Christian Ajemba sat on his metal bed in Owerri prison, on a two-inch or so mattress that had been flattened by a thousand men before him, and having finished his small supply of Flight cigarettes, made up a long, thick cigarette of his own.

He lit up, then lay back, in a shirt and socks that maybe another fifty men had worn before him, and inhaled slowly and deeply. He had not had a cigarette for weeks and the tobacco hit him hard. He was thankful he was out of his mind for a little while.

He was locked in his cell for 24 hours a day except when he was allowed to go to the toilet. He spent most of his time sewing mailbags.

He was checked every 20 minutes, even at night when he was trying to sleep. A dull red light was on in the cell 24 hours a day, so that the screws could see what he was doing every time they peered through the judas hole. Christian Ajemba thought it sheer hell trying to sleep under that red light.

He kept waking up, feeling as though he had sand in his eyes, and then he'd drop off again, only to be woken by the judas cover being pulled back. After a while, he became very ragged, never quite sure if it was night or day.

And then, suddenly, the authorities began to get paranoid. They believed highly dangerous, sophisticated and moneyed 4-1-9 mafia operatives were planning to spring Christian Ajemba from the prison, perhaps using machine-guns and even helicopters.

They started to move him around so that if anyone *did* want to help him escape, they would not know where to look. They elevated him to celebrity status, which meant that wherever he went it was always a big deal: transfers to this or that part of the prison always had to be documented in a crimson book, so that everybody knew where he was at any given time. The screws were terrified of losing him.

Christian Ajemba joked to one of the screws that he would rather lose his wife than him, and he agreed, the screw added that he'd

be sacked on the spot and, whereas he could

always find another wife, he would never ever

get a job within the prison system again.

Paranoia about Christian Ajemba got so

bad that he was moved from one cell to another

every other day or so. It got to the point where

he did not know which cell he'd be sleeping in.

The reason was obvious: they did not want him

getting too comfortable anywhere, or getting to

know people who might be bribed to send

messages out for him.

But, of course, there was no way out.

The following week he was taken to the Central

Criminal Court in Owerri in a blacked-out

armour-plated van, escorted by heavily armed

police. He was handcuffed on both sides and

locked behind doors that could be opened only by the driver.

Mr. Justice Edward Asika was again presiding. The courtroom was very heavily guarded and policed and people entering were searched for any offensive weapons.

There was a great deal of media coverage and interest. Practically all the local hotels had been booked up in advance.

Among the charged Christian Ajemba faces was complicity in the rape and killing by hanging of Patience Eze, the shooting dead of Zak, one of the vigilantes who travelled with Peter Ofondu, racketeering and international money laundering, and belonging to the 4-1-9 mafia organization.

The trial lasted two weeks. Justice Edward Asika sat without a jury for fear of 4-1-9 retaliation against jury members. The judge's summing-up took a whole day and was crushing.

Christian Ajemba stared ahead, as though the judge's words had not got to him. He felt beaten. He knew that for certain now. But he could not let his wife in the courtroom see him broken and on the floor.

The next day, just before midday, Justice Edward Asika in a crimson robe pronounced judgment: Christian Ajemba was guilty as charged.

The prosecution had again demanded exemplary 'death by firing squad' as they had earlier demanded for Godwin Diya, his half-

brother Abia and their 4-1-9 syndicate gang.

'Take him down! May the Lord have

mercy on your soul.'

The death sentences were confirmed a

week later and carried out the next day at five

o'clock in the evening by a military firing squad

in the corner of Owerri airport, the symbol of

the power of the area 4-1-9 syndicate that had

virtually run it.

The large crowd that watched fervently

hoped that spelt the beginning of the end of the

tyranny of the 4-1-9 mafia syndicate in the area.

About the Author

Dr. William Agunwa was born in Enugu, the former capital of Biafra, Eastern Nigeria.

In his early years he won an open scholarship to the prestigious Government College Umuahia and the University of Glasgow Medical School. There he qualified with a Class Prize in surgery leading to house jobs with the Regius Professors of Surgery and Medicine.

He continued training at the Royal National Orthopaedic Hospital (at both the Stanmore and London locations) and became a Senior Fellow with the Royal College of Surgeons and the Royal Society of Medicine.

From there he continued working as a consultant for teaching hospitals in England, Scotland, and the Middle East, including King Khalid Military City Hospital in Jeddah, King Abdulaziz Airforce Military Hospital in Dhahran, and Riyadh Military Teaching Hospital in Saudi Arabia. He also worked as the Chief of Surgery at King Fahad Specialist Hospital in Medina.

Besides working in the Middle East, Dr. Agunwa has also widely traveled across Europe including the Balkans, the Nordic countries, the Irish Republic, Ulster and has made several trips to the USA.

As an author, Dr. Agunwa started writing even before his medical undergraduate days with minor publications in college and parish magazines. During his career, he continued to write articles for the British Medical Journal and the Journal of Accident Surgery, going on to publish his first novel, Jobs for the Boys, in 1990.